Spot Goes to the Farm

Eric Hill

PUFFIN

Are they in the barn?

Are they in the stable?

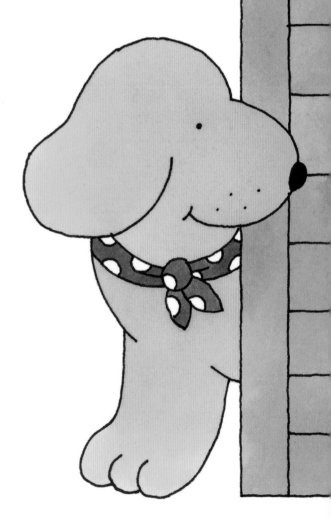

Who's that hiding behind the bush?

And who's that hiding in the straw?

Hurry up,
Spot!

Spot, get out of

the pond!

Quick, Spot, follow me!

Here they are!

Come on, Spot! There's nothing in there.

Did Dad

show you the piglets, Spot?

Yes, and then *I* found some kittens to show Dad!

PUFFIN BOOKS

Published by the Penguin Group: London, New York,
Australia, Canada, India, Ireland, New Zealand and South Africa
Penguin Books Ltd, Registered Offices:
80 Strand, London WC2R 0RL, England

puffinbooks.com

First published by William Heinemann Ltd 1987
Published in Puffin Books 1990
Reissued 2012

008

Printed and bound in China

ISBN 978–0–141–34084–5